The Strawberry Dog

Betty Paraskevas
paintings by Michael Paraskevas

Dial Books *New York*

Published by Dial Books
A Division of Penguin Books USA Inc.
375 Hudson Street
New York, New York 10014

Text copyright © 1993 by Betty Paraskevas
Paintings copyright © 1993 by Michael Paraskevas
Typography by Amelia Lau Carling
All rights reserved
Printed in Hong Kong
by South China Printing Company (1988) Limited
First Edition
1 3 5 7 9 10 8 6 4 2

Library of Congress Cataloging in Publication Data
Paraskevas, Betty.
The strawberry dog | by Betty Paraskevas ;
paintings by Michael Paraskevas. — 1st ed.
p. cm.
Summary: A homeless and independent dog and a lonely
man find companionship at a beach resort.
ISBN 0-8037-1367-3 (trade) — ISBN 0-8037-1368-1 (lib.)
[1. Dogs — Fiction. 2. Beaches — Fiction. 3. Stories in rhyme.]
I. Paraskevas, Michael, 1961–   ill. II. Title.
PZ8.3.P162St 1993 [E] — dc20 92-18216 CIP AC

The art for each picture consists of a gouache and charcoal painting,
which is scanner-separated and reproduced in full color.

To all those who love
the village of Westhampton Beach
as much as we do.
B.P. and M.P.

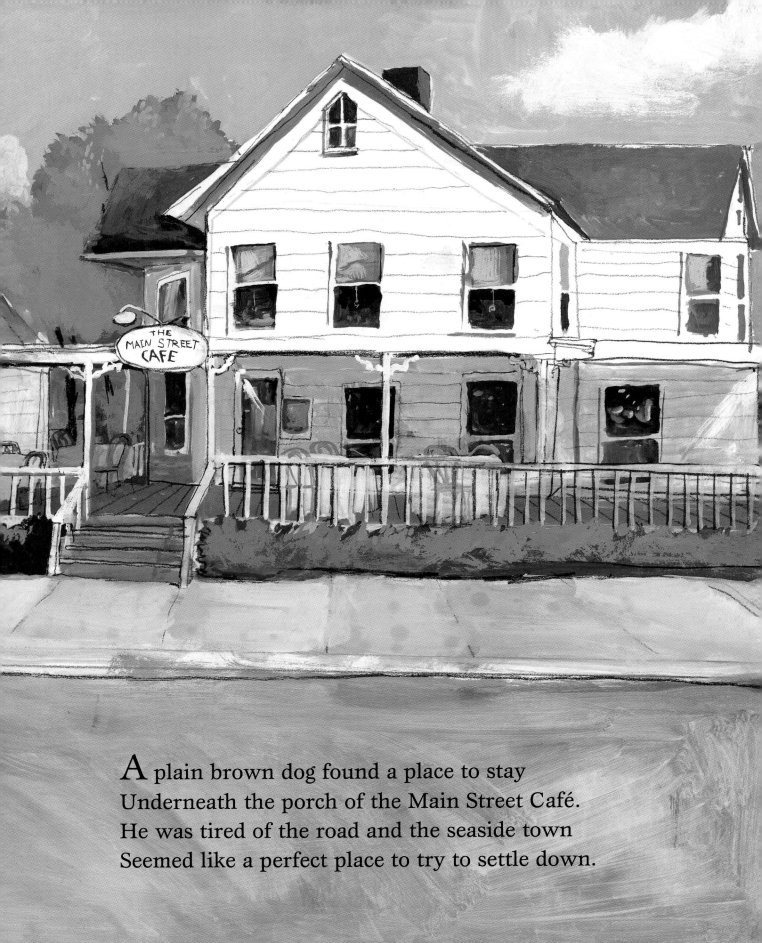

A plain brown dog found a place to stay
Underneath the porch of the Main Street Café.
He was tired of the road and the seaside town
Seemed like a perfect place to try to settle down.

He made friends with the merchants and the cop on the beat.
The sky was his ceiling, his home was the street.
They called him the Strawberry Dog for one reason,
He arrived in the middle of the strawberry season.
No one could claim him, it was easy to see,
More than anything else he loved being free.

The brothers who owned the antique store decided
He needed a bath and so they provided
An old-fashioned tub under the trees,
And they scrubbed him clean to get rid of his fleas.

The Main Street Café had the best food in town.
They served dinner on the porch when the sun went down.
There was a man who played piano, and sometimes sang a song.
One night he sang "Georgia" and the dog sang along.
The dinner guests applauded to the manager's delight,
So the man played and the dog sang "Georgia" every night.

When the last guest was gone, the Strawberry Dog would wait
At the back door for his dinner on a large paper plate.
Then he'd drift off to sleep stretched out on the ground
Underneath the porch as he listened to the sound
Of occasional footsteps, and the last thing he'd see
Were the lights going off on the movie marquee.

One warm sunny day as the clock struck four,
He met a man in front of the candy store,
And the plain brown dog who held freedom so dear
Had made a special friend, it was immediately clear.

Eli came from the city badly in need of rest.
He bought a house on the ocean and the thing he liked best
Was to drive his brand-new sandrail, and when the clock struck four
He'd pick up the plain brown dog at the candy store.

After sharing a treat they'd be on their way.
As the crowd looked on, the children would say,
"See the dog wearing goggles, strapped in his seat."
Then the sandrail took off raising dust in the street.

They'd ride along the shore 'til the sun went down.
Then Eli drove the sandrail back into town.
He'd wave good-bye as he slowly drove away,
And the dog headed back to the Main Street Café.

Sometimes Eli and the dog would take a walk
Along the main street and Eli would talk
To the merchants and summer people who'd known the dog a while,
And a very lonely man was now greeted with a smile.

The merchants were happy, the weather was divine,
Main Street was crowded, and business was just fine.
But the town by the sea was a summer town,
And when summer was over, the shops closed down.

The Main Street shopkeepers, one by one,
Locked up their stores and then followed the sun.
They were hoping that Eli would volunteer
To take care of the dog 'til they returned next year.

But Eli was restless and came to say good-bye,
He'd decided to give city life one more try.
Main Street was quiet as they shared their last cone,
Then Eli left in a taxi and the dog was all alone.

A plain brown dog without his own real name,
Waited every day but Eli never came.
The antique store would close Thanksgiving Day.
The brothers knew that before they went away,
They'd have to call the shelter, he couldn't stay alone,
But first they called Eli — no one answered the phone.

Meanwhile back in the city Eli wondered why
He'd left behind the things he loved for a two-inch view of sky.
Sitting there in his office, high on the fortieth floor,
He suddenly knew what he had to do — and he walked out the door.

The brothers watched from their window,
    the dog rose to his feet.
And they cheered when they saw the sandrail
    roar down the empty street.
It was hard to control a wagging tail
On a dog being strapped into Eli's sandrail.
But wearing his goggles, it was ready, set, go,
And as the friends waved good-bye, it began to snow.

This is the story as it was told to me,
By Eli who lives in a house by the sea,
Where friends share his fire on cold winter nights,
And he's found success with the books that he writes.

His plain brown dog is always by his side,
Sometimes they walk and sometimes they ride.
He's a dog anyone would proudly claim,
But he's Eli's dog and Sam is his name.

DATE DUE

MAR 14 '96			
NOV 1 1 96			
JAN 02 '97			
APR 03 '97			
OCT 2 0 '97			
NOV 7 6 97			
DEC 03 2008			
GAYLORD			PRINTED IN U.S.A.